Book 4: VISION of PEARLS

CLAIRVOYANT CLAIRE

Spellbound

An Imprint of Magic Wagon
abdobooks.com

BY JENNY SCOTT   ILLUSTRATED BY BILLY YONG

FOR GAVIN AND BELLA -JS

TO RACHEL, FOR ALWAYS BELIEVING IN ME -BY

abdobooks.com

Published by Magic Wagon, a division of ABDO, PO Box 398166, Minneapolis, Minnesota 55439. Copyright © 2020 by Abdo Consulting Group, Inc. International copyrights reserved in all countries. No part of this book may be reproduced in any form without written permission from the publisher. Spellbound™ is a trademark and logo of Magic Wagon.

Printed in the United States of America, North Mankato, Minnesota.

102019
012020

Written by Jenny Scott
Illustrated by Billy Yong
Edited by Tamara L. Britton
Art Directed by Christina Doffing and Laura Graphenteen

Library of Congress Control Number: 2019942290

Publisher's Cataloging-in-Publication Data

Names: Scott, Jenny, author. | Yong, Billy, illustrator.
Title: Vision of pearls / by Jenny Scott ; illustrated by Billy Yong.
Description: Minneapolis, Minnesota : Magic Wagon, 2020. | Series: Clairvoyant Claire; book 4
Summary: Twelve-year-old Olivia is psychic! She sees in a vision that the police are searching for a missing necklace. Olivia and her friend Sebastian contact the police through their blog Clairvoyant Claire. With Olivia and Sebastian's help the police solve the mystery, find the necklace, and arrest the culprit.
Identifiers: ISBN 9781532136597 (lib. bdg.) | ISBN 9781532137198 (ebook) | ISBN 9781532137495 (Read-to-Me ebook)
Subjects: LCSH: Clairvoyants--Juvenile fiction. | Blogs--Juvenile fiction. | Jewelry--Juvenile fiction. | Jewelry theft--Juvenile fiction. | Mystery and detective stories--Juvenile fiction. | Friendship--Juvenile fiction. | Self-confidence--Juvenile fiction.
Classification: DDC [Fic]--dc23

Table of Contents

CHAPTER 1
Call for Help

Sebastian and I are in the park

THROWING a Frisbee for

my goldendoodle, Rocky, when

GOOSE BUMPS

prickle along my arms.

The park disappears and a VISION

zips into my head.

Suddenly, I'm in the Edgewood Police Department STANDING behind Officer Ezra. She's at her desk POURING over an open file. There's a note on the top that says, *Missing Montwood pearl necklace* and another that says *House is haunted?*

6

Officer Ezra MUTTERS, "Maybe I should call Clairvoyant Claire because this case is going nowhere real QUICK."

8

When I come back to the park, the SUN is shining in my eyes. I SQUINT and look at Sebastian.

"New VISION?" he says.

"Yup." I whistle for Rocky and he comes **galloping** over, the Frisbee clamped between his teeth. "I think Officer Ezra needs our **HELP**."

At home, Sebastian logs into the *Clairvoyant Claire* blog. He's a **FAST** typer so he writes while I speak.

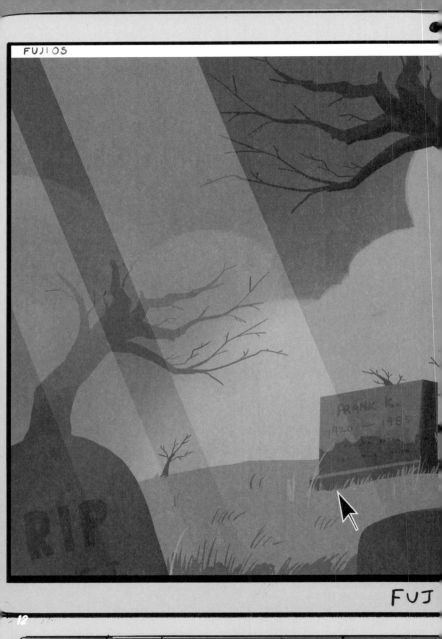

CLAIRVOYANT CLAIRE

Dear Officer Ezra,

You should **call** me. I don't know much about **ghosts**, but I do think I can help you **FIND** the missing necklace if you give me a chance.

Sincerely,

Clairvoyant Claire

CHAPTER 2
The Missing Pearls

Officer Ezra **knocks** on my door that afternoon. "How did you know I was *searching* for a necklace?"

"A VISION."

She **NARROWS** her eyes like she's trying to decide if I'm telling tales. "Well, Clairvoyant Claire. I *do* need your **HELP**."

"That is Montwood Mansion," Officer Ezra says. "And you're *right*, Sebastian. I had **TWO** officers in that house yesterday. They claim to have saw a **ghostly** figure dressed in clothing from another era."

"What does the house have to do with the necklace?" I ask.

"Since Mrs. Montwood's DEATH, her PEARL necklace has been missing. It's worth a fortune. Her daughter, Peggy, and son, Jonathan, swear it's in the house, but no one has been able to locate it. The ghost certainly doesn't help."

Officer Ezra pulls a gold pocket watch with a LONG chain from her jacket. "This was Mrs. Montwood's other prized possession. Sebastian said you had a VISION at the theater when you touched a hairbrush?"

"Yes. But I'm not **sure** if I can do it again."

"It's worth trying," Sebastian says.

I *REACH* for the watch. As my fingers touch the cold metal, **GOOSE BUMPS** pop on my arms.

In my VISION, I'm in a closet surrounded by glittering dresses. A woman kneels on the floor and pushes the dresses aside to reveal a hidden compartment in the wall. Lying inside is a shiny PEARL necklace.

CHAPTER 3
Montwood Mansion

Officer Ezra **drives** us over to

Montwood Mansion in her police car.

She has to OPEN the back

door for us after we park in the

CIRCULAR driveway.

Inside, the mansion is **dark** and still. Dusty sheets cover the furniture. **COBWEBS** hang from the ceiling. Sebastian **clings** to my arm as we make our way up the **WINDING** staircase. At the top of the stairs, we go **DOWN** the main hallway and pass several bedrooms.

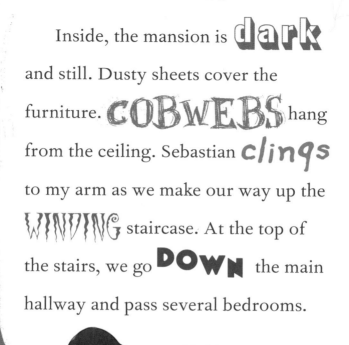

Something **MOVES** out of the corner of my **EYE**.

The floor creaks.

We all turn around and see a pale figure *looming* toward us!

Sebastian SCREAMS.

Officer Ezra urges us down the hall. "Here, INSIDE! This is Mrs. Montwood's room."

"It really is **HAUNTED**!" Sebastian says. He tries the **LIGHT** switch, but it doesn't work so Officer Ezra clicks on her flashlight. The bed is still made like it's **waiting** for Mrs. Montwood to come back to it.

Dust **SWIRLS** in the light.

"Hurry, Olivia," Officer Ezra says. "Where do we **LOOK**?"

I find the closet. Officer Ezra **SWEEPS** her flashlight over the hanging dresses.

31

"This is it," I say. I **kneel** on the floor just like I saw Mrs. Montwood do in my VISION. I shove aside the dresses and run my hand over the wall. I feel a little metal latch and **PULL** it open.

Officer Ezra and Sebastian **kneel** beside me. The flashlight beam *shining* in the hidden compartment reveals a set of shiny **PEARLS**.

"You've found them!" Officer Ezra says.

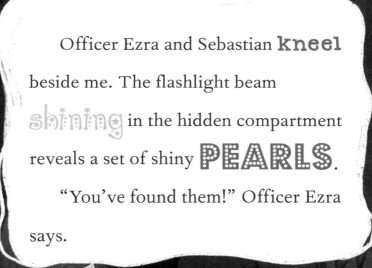

I **PULL** them from the hiding spot and hold them up to the **LIGHT**. That's when the *ghost* swoops in from the doorway and snatches them away.

CHAPTER 4
Town Heroes

"**Ghost**!" Sebastian shouts.

"That's no **ghost**. That's

Jonathan Montwood,"

Officer Ezra

says.

The man is dressed in a dusty soldier's uniform. White makeup on his face makes him look PALE.

"I've been LOOKING for this necklace for a very long time," he says. "I didn't want my sister to get her grubby hands on it. I had to pretend to be a ghost to keep people away while I searched."

39

"Those aren't yours to take," Officer Ezra says.

"And what are you going to do about it?" He turns and runs, but Sebastian sticks out his foot and TRIPS him. The PEARLS go flying!

I reach out and SNATCH them safely from the air.

"Jonathan Montwood," Officer Ezra says, "you are under ARREST."

"Those PEARLS are mine!" Jonathan yells. "I DESERVE them more than my sister!"

Back at the police department, Peggy Montwood takes the PEARLS with tears in her EYES. "I wanted my brother and I to share our mother's heirlooms, but he just wanted to sell them. I'm so glad the pearls have been found." She looks at us. "How did you know where to LOOK?"

"We had **HELP** from Clairvoyant Claire," Sebastian says. "We're very good **friends** with her."

POLICE DEPARTMEN

"Oh, I just *love* Clairvoyant Claire's blog!" Peggy says. "I've been following since the beginning. Please tell her **thank you** for me."

"We will," Sebastian says.

"She's always **HAPPY** to help," I say.

Officer Ezra *WINKS* at me. "Clairvoyant Claire is one of Edgewood's finest **HEROES**."